TEENAGE MUTANT NINJA TURTLES™
NEW ANIMATED ADVENTURES
VOLUME 1

STORY: **KENNY BYERLY**
ART: **DARIO BRIZUELA**
COLORS: **HEATHER BRECKEL**
LETTERS: **SHAWN LEE**
EDITS: **BOBBY CURNOW**

 Spotlight

ABDOPUBLISHING.COM

Reinforced library bound edition published in 2016 by Spotlight, a division of ABDO
PO Box 398166, Minneapolis, Minnesota 55439. Spotlight produces high-quality
reinforced library bound editions for schools and libraries.
Published by agreement with IDW.

Printed in the United States of America, North Mankato, Minnesota.
092015
012016

CATALOGING-IN-PUBLICATION DATA

Byerly, Kenny.
 Teenage Mutant Ninja Turtles : new animated adventures / writer, Kenny Byerly ; illustrator, Dario
Brizuela. -- Reinforced library bound edition.
  p. cm. (Teenage Mutant Ninja Turtles : new animated adventures)
Volumes 1-2 written by Kenny Byerly ; illustrated by Dario Brizuela. -- Volume 3 written by Scott
Tipton, David Tipton, and Kenny Byerly ; illustrated by Dario Brizuela. -- Volume 4 written by Erik
Burnham ; illustrated by Dario Brizuela.
Summary: Spinning straight out of the hit Nickelodeon show, a fantastic tale takes the Turtles on a
dangerous rescue mission.
ISBN 978-1-61479-459-2 (vol. 1) -- ISBN 978-1-61479-460-8 (vol. 2) -- ISBN 978-1-61479-461-5
(vol. 3) -- ISBN 978-1-61479-462-2 (vol. 4)
1. Teenage Mutant Ninja Turtles (Fictitious characters)--Juvenile fiction.
2. Superheroes--Juvenile fiction. 3. Adventure and adventurers--Juvenile fiction. 4. Graphic
novels--Juvenile fiction. I. Brizuela, Dario, illustrator. II. Tipton, Scott, author. III. Tipton, David,
author. IV. Burnham, Erik, author. V. Title.
741.5--dc23

2015955128

Spotlight

A Division of ABDO
abdopublishing.com

SHE CAN HANDLE IT, LEO. WE'LL JUST PICK UP A *DIODE MODULE* FOR MY NEW *INVENTION*.

NO *COMBAT*. JUST A LITTLE *STEALTH*.

YEAH! WHICH I KICKED *BUTT* AT TODAY!

I WOULDN'T GO *THAT* FAR. MIKEY STILL *SPOTTED* YOU.

YOU DIDN'T SPOT ME.

OOH, *BURN!* SHE *WENT* THERE!

LEO, IT'S *FINE.* I'VE NEVER HAD A PROBLEM AT THE JUNKYARD BEFORE.

YOU NEVER BROUGHT *APRIL* BEFORE!

HEY!

THAT'S *IT.* COME ON, DONNIE. LET'S GO.

THANKS, DONNIE. THIS IS GONNA BE *FUN*.

NO TRESPASSING

NO TRESPASSING

YOU *BET*. WHAT'S WITH THE *WIG*?

SHADOWS AREN'T THE ONLY WAY TO HIDE.

SPLINTER SAYS A TRUE *KUNOICHI* USES *DECEPTION* TO HIDE IN PLAIN SIGHT.

NO TRESPASSING

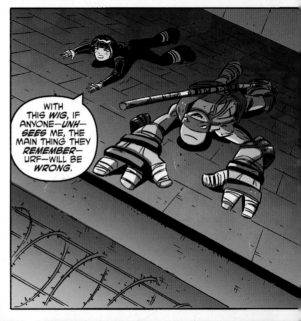

WITH THIS *WIG*, IF ANYONE—*UNH*—SEES ME, THE MAIN THING THEY *REMEMBER*—URF—WILL BE *WRONG*.

WELL, IF ANYONE SEES *ME*, NO ONE'S GOING TO BE TALKING ABOUT YOUR *HAIR*.

SCRRTCH

SO LET'S SAVE HIDING IN *PLAIN SIGHT* FOR ANOTHER DAY, AND JUST STICK WITH REGULAR OLD HIDING IN THE *SHADOWS*.

WHAT'S YOUR *NAME*?

I *TOLD* YOU, IT'S JANUARY MCANDREWS!

SURE IT IS. WHO ARE YOU WORKING FOR, MS. MCANDREWS?

NO ONE! I ONLY SNUCK IN HERE BECAUSE MY STUPID FRIENDS *DARED* ME!

AND DID YOUR "FRIENDS" ALSO *DARE* YOU TO TAKE HIGHLY SPECIFIC COMPONENTS FROM OUR *EQUIPMENT*?

WHAT, THAT? ISN'T IT ALL JUST *JUNK*?

THIS IS A *TOP SECRET* GOVERNMENT FACILITY. YOU EXPECT ME TO BELIEVE YOU DIDN'T *REALIZE* THAT?

WHAT? NO WAY! I'M JUST MESSING AROUND!

YOU KNOW HOW *TEENAGERS* ARE! WITH OUR *LOUD MUSIC* AND NO RESPECT FOR *RULES!* WE'RE THE WORST!

YES...

BUT *MOST* TEENAGERS DON'T CARRY AROUND *CUSTOM CELL PHONES* AND *NINJA WEAPONS.*

HEH. NINJA WEAPONS? WHAT NINJA WEAPONS?! THAT'S... UM... *JEWELRY!*

DONNIE, *PLEASE* BE WORKING ON A *PLAN*...

HEY, THIS PLACE *IS* COOL! HOW COME YOU NEVER INVITED *ME?* YOU *KNOW* HOW MUCH I LOVE JUNK!

WAY TO *GO*, DONNIE. EVERYONE KNOWS THE WAY TO A GIRL'S *HEART* IS TO GET HER CAPTURED BY THE *ARMY.*

THIS IS SERIOUS, RAPH. WHERE'S *APRIL?*

THEY'VE GOT HER IN *THERE.*

BIG DEAL. WE'VE FACED DOWN GIANT *MUTANT MONSTERS.* THESE GUYS DON'T LOOK SO *TOUGH.*

THE *DIFFERENCE* IS, THESE AREN'T *BAD GUYS.* WE DON'T WANT TO HURT THEM.

BUT IF THEY *SEE* US, THE *GOVERNMENT'S* GONNA WANT TO KNOW MORE ABOUT US.

THEN THEY'LL JUST HAVE TO READ MY *BLOG!*

YOU HAVE A *BLOG?!*

MIKEY! OUR EXISTENCE IS A *SECRET,* REMEMBER?!

IT'S *OKAY!* I JUST TALK ABOUT *TV SHOWS!*

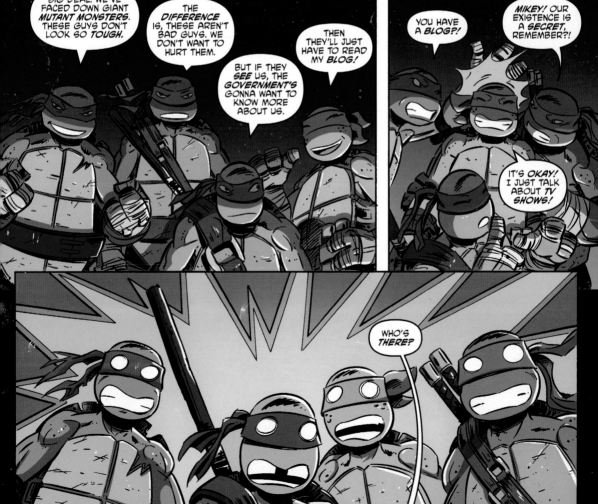

WHO'S *THERE?*

ALL UNITS FLANK THE XJ-17 LASER CANNON!

NICE, APRIL.

APRIL? WHERE?

SHE'S STILL IN THERE, BUT SHE'S CLEARING US A *PATH*.

PAF

CRASH

BREACH! BREACH!

DEET

THE *FORECAST* FOR TODAY IS... *CLOUDY!*

YOU JUST CAN'T *HELP* YOURSELF, CAN YOU?

THIS WAY—*GAH!*

NOT SO FAST!

T-PHONE SELF-DESTRUCT!

POW

THWACK

BOOYAKASHAAAAA!

THOCK

FZZT

GAH!

AGAIN, *REAL* SORRY!

...BOOYAKASHA?

KILL THE *LIGHTS!*

I'M ON IT!

HUH. I WAS KINDA HOPING IT'D BE *DARKER.*

YEAH, ME TOO.

IT'S *OKAY.* WE CAN TAKE THESE GUYS.

SURE, IF WE WANT THE *GOVERNMENT* TO BE HUNTING US ALONG WITH THE KRAANG AND THE FOOT CLAN.

AND SNAKEWEED AND SPIDER-BYTEZ AND BAXTER STOCKMAN AND...

OKAY, WE HAVE A LOT OF ENEMIES! I *GET* IT!

TROMP TROMP TROMP TROMP

BEING A *BRUNETTE* DIDN'T SUIT ME ANYWAY.

DEET

PHEW.

CLICK

ALL RIGHT. LET'S TURN ON THE *DARK.*